Tales from Duckport®

Back to School?
Cool!

by Suzy Spafford

SCHOLASTIC INC.

New York Toronto London Auckland Sydney
Mexico City New Delhi Hong Kong Buenos Aires

ISBN 0-439-38355-2

Cover design by Keirsten Geise.
Interior design by Robin Camera.

10 9 8 7 6 5 4 3 2 1   02 03 04   05

Printed in the U.S.A.
First Scholastic printing, August 2002

TABLE OF CONTENTS

Many, many years ago, two brothers discovered the Beak Isles. Their names were Tim Duck One and Tim Duck Two. Tim Duck Two started the town of Duckport there. To this day, pictures of this fearless explorer can be seen all over town. How many can you find?

THE NEW KID

It was the first day of school in Duckport.

"Now I look like a second grader,"
Suzy Ducken declared.

Suzy and her best friend, Emily
Marmot, walked to school together.
Emily kept pulling hair bows out
of her bag.
"What do you think?" she asked
Suzy. "I can't decide which one to
wear."

7

"I think you're driving me crazy!"
Suzy giggled.
Jack Quacker zipped past them on
his skateboard.
"Woo-hoo!" he shouted.
"Second grader coming through!"

"Look out!" Suzy called.

Jack whipped around a little girl.

"Oh, no!" said Suzy.

"That's my new neighbor, Penelope
O'Quinn."

"Are you okay, Penelope?" Suzy asked.

"I'm all right," Penelope answered shyly.

Emily helped Penelope pick up her lunch.

There were olives, a tuna-and-marshmallow sandwich, and a green banana.

How odd, thought Emily. *She* had a jelly sandwich cut into neat triangles.

Suzy thought Penelope's lunch looked interesting. "Want to walk to school with us?" Suzy asked Penelope.

"That would be nice,"
said Penelope.
Secretly, she was thinking,
That would be great!
She hadn't made any new
Duckport friends yet.

"I can't wait to meet our new teacher," Suzy said.

"I brought her something," Penelope said in her soft voice. "See?"

"It sure is . . . thorny,"
Emily remarked.
"Thank you!"
replied
Penelope.
"I wanted
to get her
something
that no one
else would."

Suzy smiled.
"I only brought
her a boring old
apple!"

At the school yard, the girls joined
a jump-rope game.
"Let's do the bubble gum song,"
called Suzy.
Suddenly a voice boomed,

BUBBLE GUM, BUBBLE GUM, IN A DISH.
HOW MANY PIECES DO YOU WISH?
ONE . . . TWO . . . THREE . . .

. . .FOUR. . .FIVE. . .SIX. . .
Windows rattled.
Traffic stopped.
Penelope sure was full of surprises!

GETTING TO KNOW YOU

Everyone was anxious to meet
the new teacher.

"I wonder if she's funny," said Jack.

"I wonder if she's strict," said
Corky Turtle.

"I wonder why she's not here
yet," said Suzy.

Just then, the loud *BRRIIIIINNGG!*
of a bicycle bell rang behind them.
"Sorry I'm late!" the teacher sang
out. "I stopped for doughnuts!
Nothing kicks off the school year
like a good cruller, I always say!"

"I am Ms. Cornelia O'Plume,"
she announced. "But if you
like, you may call me Ms. O."

Ms. O pulled some very odd
things out of her bag.
"Well, boys and girls," Ms.
O'Plume began.
"We have a very exciting year
ahead of us."

"We are going to keep journals.
We are going to work with fractions.
And we are even going to build a
city out of snack crackers."

"Sometimes," Ms. O'Plume said,
"we will stand on our heads. But
mostly, we are going to HAVE FUN!"

"Now it's your turn.
Suzy Ducken, would you please tell
us about yourself?" Ms. O asked.
"Certainly, Ms. O'Plume," replied
Suzy. Folks always noticed her good
manners.
Ms. O did, too.

Suzy described her rock collection.

Then Jack performed his latest skateboard move.

Corky talked about
his interest in maps.
He especially liked
Ms. O's globe
earrings.

Emily skipped her turn.
She was busy handing out napkins.
"Doughnuts can be so messy!"
she observed.

Finally, it was Penelope's turn.
"My favorite color is brown, because
it goes with *me*," she began.
"And my favorite snack is stuffed
olives—because I like food that
looks you in the eye!"

Then she added, "And I like being
a porcupine because I can put stuff
on my quills!"
Her classmates laughed.
Who *was* this new kid, anyway?

"Ms. O'Plume?" Suzy asked.
"What were *you* like in school?"
"Let's say I had an unusual way
of looking at things," Ms. O said.
Then she turned and gave Penelope
a great big smile.

A BIG FAN

The students in Ms. O'Plume's class were wiggling. And it was exactly what Ms. O had asked them to do! Doing the "Jell-O dance" was how everyone warmed up for art.

Ms. O'Plume divided the class
into three groups.
She gave each group some very
unusual art supplies.

"I would like you to create your very own leaf art," Ms. O instructed. "Think about expressing the beauty of the season in a whole new way! No idea is a bad idea."

"Let's think of something really cool," Suzy said to her friends. "Let's wait and see what everybody else is doing," said Jack. "That's a bad idea." Emily scowled. Jack replied, "But Ms. O said there are no bad ideas!"

"Trust me!" Suzy insisted. "Copying is *always* a bad idea."

"I know what we could make," Penelope offered.

Everyone listened as she softly told her plan.

All the groups were hard at work.
Finally, Ms. O called out, "Finish
up, kids! It's show time!"

Vivian Snortwood's group went first.
"We put the leaves under the paper
and rubbed the crayons on the top,"
Vivian explained.
"Very nice," Ms. O remarked.
"I love the colors!"

The next group unrolled their paper.
The trees on their picture were
covered with real leaves.
"I like the way you used those leaves,"
said Ms. O'Plume.
"Next group!"

Suzy and her friends made a pile
of leaves in the middle of the floor.
Penelope paused dramatically, then
announced, "I give you . . . FALL!"
Jack turned on the ceiling fan.

The leaves swirled all around.
It was like being outside on a
windy day!
The children and Ms. O'Plume
erupted into applause.
"Bravo!" said Ms. O.
"Living art! How original!"

As they cleaned up the leaves,
Jack told Penelope,
"Your idea was really different,
but it turned out great!"
"Penelope's ideas *are* different,"
Suzy said. "And *that's* what we
like about her!"